MAX AND THE SUPERHEROES

Rocio Bonilla & Oriol Malet

ini Charlesbridge

Like most kids his age, Max is crazy about superheroes.

When he was really little, he anxiously
awaited Halloween for the chance to dress
up as a superhero. But now he realizes that
he doesn't need a special occasion.

He is fascinated by the stories that his grandpa Joe tells him. They are old-timey tales of superheroes who rescue cats in danger. They are so brave!

Max's friends are crazy about superheroes, too.

Leo loves Silver Snake, who stars in a video game.
Martin dreams of growing up to be Black Machine.
Emma likes the movie that features Red Force.

Max reads every comic book he can get his hands on.

He thinks his friends' favorite superheroes are awesome, but there is one that is his clear favorite.

MEGA POWER

Martin says that there is no way a woman superhero can be that strong. Max doesn't care what Martin thinks. Max is sure that Megapower is different from all the other superheroes.

MEGAPOWER DOESN'T JUST RESCUE CATS, LIKE IN GRANDPA JOE'S STORIES. SHE CAN ALSO TAME ANY ANIMAL, NO MATTER HOW BIG OR FIERCE.

SHE IS SUPER INTELLIGENT. SHE IS SO SMART THAT SHE CAN DECIPHER ANY SECRET CODE, NO MATTER HOW COMPLICATED.

OF COURSE, MEGAPOWER CAN FLY. SHE TRAVELS TO THE FARTHEST REACHES OF THE PLANET. AND BEST OF ALL, SHE OFTEN TAKES MAX WITH HER TO SHOW HIM ALL THOSE FABULOUS PLACES.

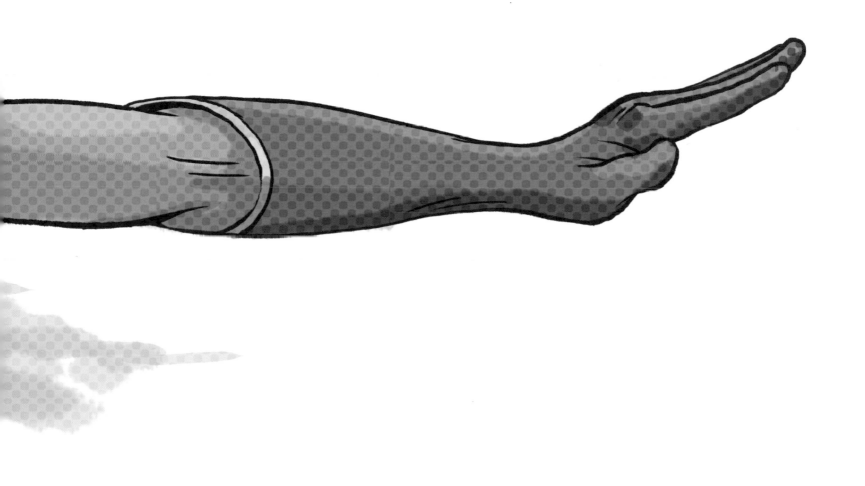

How can that be? Because Max knows Megapower!

Actually, the truth is . . .

the best thing about Megapower . . .

isn't that she can deactivate bombs
and control a million robots at once.

It isn't her X-ray vision, which can see through everything. (Honestly, ultravision isn't all that cool.)

It's not that she can decipher any secret code, no matter how complicated.

It isn't that she can rescue cats
and tame animals, either.

There's no denying that saving people
and taking Max flying is awesome. But . . .

the very best thing
about Megapower is,
without a doubt . . .

when she puts on her Mommy costume
and gives Max a kiss good night.

TO GUILLEM, FOR BEING THERE EVERY DAY AND SHARING
THIS EXTRAORDINARY ADVENTURE WITH ME—R. B.

TO MERITXELL, MY MEGAPOWER—O. M.

2018 First US Edition
Translation copyright © 2016 by Mara Lethem
All rights reserved, including the right of reproduction in whole or in part in any form.
Charlesbridge and colophon are registered trademarks of Charlesbridge Publishing, Inc.

At the time of publication, any URLs printed in this book were accurate
and active. Charlesbridge and the author are not responsible for the
content or accessibility of any website.

Published by Charlesbridge
85 Main Street
Watertown, MA 02472
(617) 926-0329
www.charlesbridge.com

First published in Spain in 2016 by Edicions Bromera, S. L. Alzira, as Max i els superherois
www.bromera.com
Text copyright © 2016 by Rocio Bonilla
Illustrations copyright © 2016 by Rocio Bonilla and Oriol Malet
Copyright © Edicions Bromera, S. L. Alzira, 2016

Library of Congress Cataloging-in-Publication Data
Names: Bonilla, Rocio, 1970- author, illustrator. | Malet, Oriol,
    illustrator. | Lethem, Mara, translator.
Title: Max and the superheroes / Rocio Bonilla & Oriol Malet.
Other titles: Max i els superherois. English
Description: First US edition. | Watertown, MA : Charlesbridge, [2018] |
    "First published in Spain in 2016 by Edicions Bromera, S. L. Alzira, as
    Max I els superherois." | "Illustrations copyright 2016 by Rocio Bonilla
    and Oriol Malet" | "Translation copyright 2016 by Mara Lethem" |
Summary:
    Max is crazy about superheroes, like all his friends, but the one he loves
    most is Megapower—especially when she turns into his Mommy and gives
    him a goodnight kiss.
Identifiers: LCCN 2017042930 (print) | LCCN 2017045907 (ebook) |
    ISBN 9781632897442 (ebook) | ISBN 9781632897459 (ebook pdf) |
    ISBN 9781580898447 (reinforced for library use)
Subjects: LCSH: Superheroes—Juvenile fiction. | Mothers and sons—Juvenile
    fiction. | CYAC: Superheroes—Fiction. | Mothers and sons—Fiction. |
    LCGFT: Picture books.
Classification: LCC PZ7.1.B669 (ebook) | LCC PZ7.1.B669 Max 2018 (print) |
    DDC [E]—dc23
LC record available at https://lccn.loc.gov/2017042930

Printed in China
(hc) 10 9 8 7 6 5 4 3 2 1

Display type set in Suspicion by Scriptorium Fonts
Text type set in Gotham by Hoefler & Frere-Jones and Blambot by Blambot
Printed by 1010 Printing International Limited in Huizhou, Guangdong, China
Production supervision by Brian G. Walker
Designed by Sarah Richards Taylor